For Molly Melling
Thanks Mum

JUST LIKE MY MUM
by David Melling

British Library Cataloguing in Publication Data
A catalogue record of this book is available from the British Library.

ISBN 0 340 86090 1

Copyright © David Melling 2004

The right of David Melling to be identified as the author and illustrator
of this Work has been asserted by him in accordance with
the Copyright, Designs and Patents Act 1988.

First edition published 2004
10 9 8 7 6 5 4 3 2 1

Published by Hodder Children's Books
a division of Hodder Headline Limited
338 Euston Road London NW1 3BH

Printed in Italy

11

Just Like My Mum

David Melling

Hodder
Children's
Books

A division of Hodder Headline Limited

This is my mum.

In the morning I always wake early...

...just like my mum.

I y-a-w-n,

and g*rrr*oan,

and I'm ready
for the day...

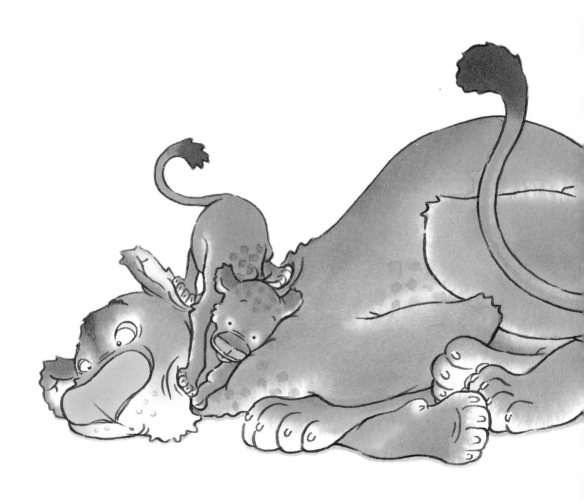

...just like my mum.

If I hurt myself,

or argue with
someone,

or get upset...

...my mum makes me feel better.

And when
I'm a cheeky
little monkey…

I say 'sorry'...

...just like my mum.

When I'm bored my mum
doesn't like it.

She says,

'Why don't you do something?'

But when I do something…

she says,

'Just sit still
for five
minutes!'

My mum helps
me make things.
She knows
everything.

And her ideas are *so* interesting…

...everyone wants to play!

Sometimes I have good
ideas of my own...

Then Mum says,
'*Dry games are better!*'

That's typical…

...just like
my mum.

There's an old squiggly
tree which is my
favourite place
for climbing with
my friends.

But at the end of the day,
we all want to be somewhere
quiet, safe and warm,
with someone...

...just like
my mum.

Other books by David Melling:

Cartwheels in the Kitchen

The Kiss That Missed

Jack Frost

Just Like My Dad

Also illustrated by David Melling:

What's That Noise?

Gerda the Goose

Jump In!

All Change!

Gently Bentley!

Count Down to Bedtime

Are You Ready?

First Adventures of Fidget and Quilly

The Adventures of Harry